THE ADVENTURES OF FELUDA

SEVEN THRILLING CASES

ABHISEK BOSE

Made with ♥ on the Notion Press Platform
www.notionpress.com

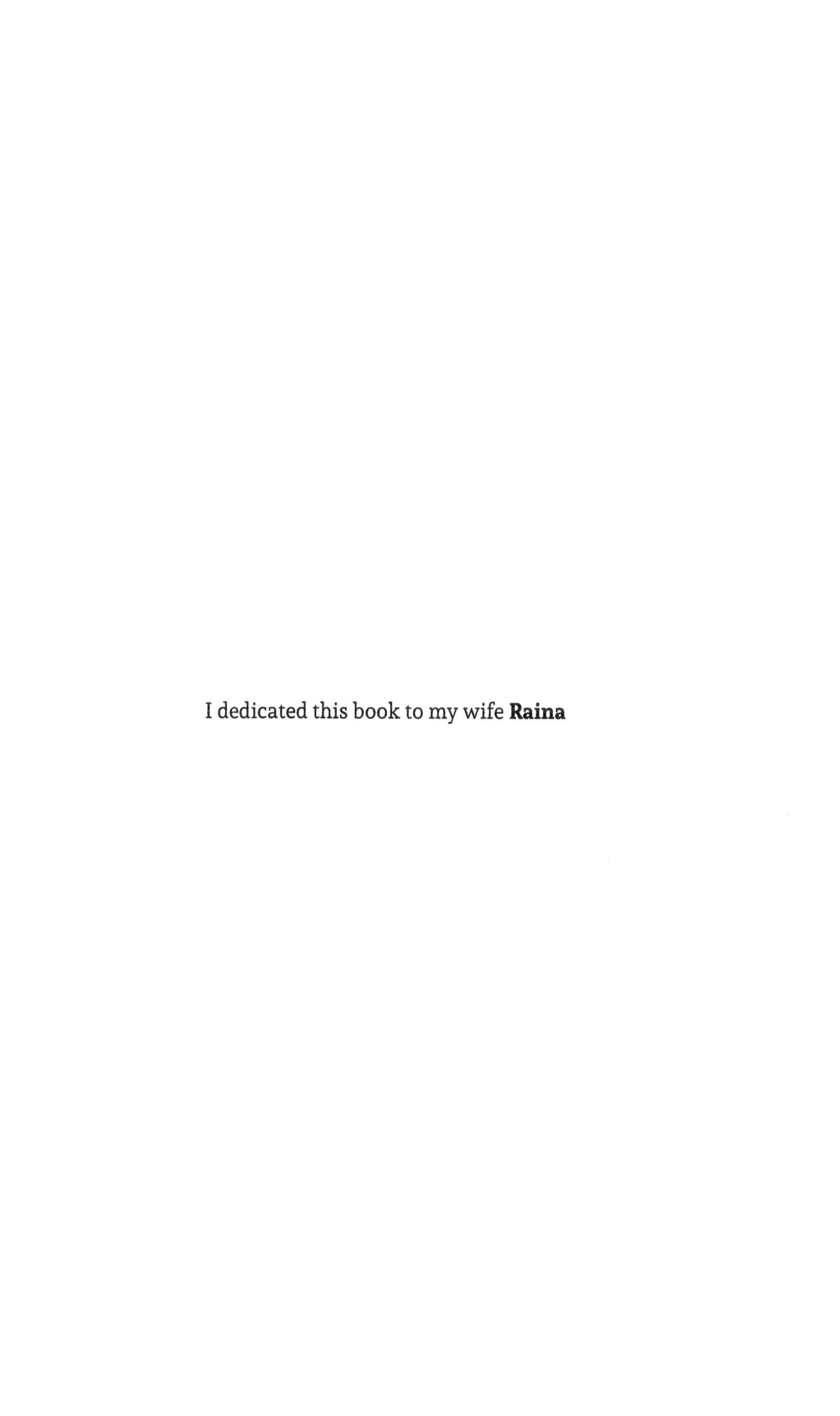

I dedicated this book to my wife **Raina**

Contents

ONE

The Haunting of Feluda and the Enigma of the Abandoned Mansion

Chapter 1: The Haunted Mansion

Feluda, Topshe, and Lalmohan Babu were driving down a deserted road on the outskirts of Kolkata. They had received a call from a friend who claimed to have seen a ghost in a mansion on this road. As they approached the mansion, the three friends felt a chill run down their spines. The mansion was dark and foreboding, with vines crawling up the walls and broken windows.

As they entered the mansion, they found themselves in a large hall, with cobwebs hanging from the ceiling and a musty smell in the air. Feluda took out his flashlight and started looking around for clues. Suddenly, they heard a strange noise coming from upstairs. They quickly made their way up the stairs, with Lalmohan Babu muttering to himself about the foolishness of chasing ghosts.

As they reached the top of the stairs, they heard the noise again. It sounded like a faint whisper, but they couldn't make out what it was saying. Feluda motioned for the others to stay behind as he cautiously made his way down the hallway. Suddenly, a door creaked open and a shadowy figure appeared.

Chapter 2: The Ghostly Encounter

The shadowy figure turned out to be a young woman, with long hair and a pale complexion. She introduced herself as Maya and explained that she was the granddaughter of the mansion's owner, who had passed away a few months ago. Maya told the three friends that she had been hearing strange noises in the mansion since her grandfather's death, and she was convinced that the mansion was haunted.

Feluda, Topshe, and Lalmohan Babu listened to Maya's story with interest. Feluda, in particular, was intrigued by the idea of a haunted mansion. He asked Maya if she had seen any ghosts, but she replied that she had only heard strange noises.

Feluda decided to investigate further. He asked Maya to show him the room where she had heard the noises. As they walked down the hallway, Feluda noticed that the air had grown colder and there was a strange smell in the air.

Chapter 3: The Secret Room

Maya led Feluda, Topshe, and Lalmohan Babu to a room at the end of the hallway. The room was locked, and Maya didn't have the key. Feluda examined the lock and realized that it was a simple one. He took out a bobby pin and quickly picked the lock.

As the door creaked open, the three friends gasped in surprise. The room was filled with strange artifacts and symbols. There was a large pentagram on the floor and strange symbols on the walls. Feluda examined the symbols and realized that they were from an ancient civilization.

Suddenly, they heard a strange noise coming from a corner of the room. They turned around and saw a small creature huddled in the corner. The creature had large, glowing eyes and a scaly body. Feluda realized that they were dealing with something far more dangerous than a ghost.

Chapter 4: The Alien Encounter

The creature slowly approached the three friends, its eyes fixed on them. Feluda quickly realized that the creature was an alien and that it had been trapped in the mansion for years. He spoke to the creature in a strange language, and the creature responded.

Feluda learned that the alien had been stranded on Earth for years, and had been searching for a way to return to its home planet. It had stumbled upon the mansion and had been trying to use the symbols and artifacts in the room to create a portal back to its home planet.

As they walked through the dark and spooky woods, Feluda noticed that Topshe seemed to be shivering with fear.

"What's wrong Topshe?" he asked.

"It's just that this place gives me the creeps," replied Topshe. "I can't shake off this feeling of dread."

Feluda smiled. "You're a grown man now, Topshe. Surely you're not still scared of the dark?"

"It's not just the dark, Feluda," said Topshe. "It's this place. Something about it just feels off."

Feluda nodded thoughtfully. He knew that there was a reason why they had been called to this remote part of the country and that it was likely to be something strange and mysterious. But he didn't want to alarm Topshe any further.

They soon arrived at the old mansion that had been their destination. It was a sprawling building with large, creaky doors and ivy-covered walls. As they entered, Feluda noticed that the air was heavy and oppressive, as if there was a weight on his chest.

They were greeted by the owner of the mansion, a wealthy man named Ramen Dutta. He was a short, portly man with a round face and thinning hair. "Welcome, Feluda," he said. "Thank you for coming at such short notice."

Feluda nodded. "Of course, Mr Dutta. What seems to be the problem?"

"It's my daughter," said Dutta. "She's been acting strange lately. She's become withdrawn and distant, and she keeps talking about seeing things that aren't there."

Feluda raised an eyebrow. "What kind of things?"

Dutta hesitated. "I'm not sure. She says there are...creatures...in the house. She says they come to her at night and whisper in her ear."

Feluda exchanged a knowing look with Topshe. "We'll take a look around and see what we can find," he said.

As they began to investigate, Feluda noticed that there was something decidedly eerie about the mansion. The walls seemed to be alive with whispers and the floorboards creaked as if underfoot of something else. And then, as they entered the room where Dutta's daughter slept, they both heard a strange and unsettling sound.

It was a soft hissing noise, like the sound of snakes slithering. Feluda followed the sound to a small cupboard in the corner of the room. When he opened the door, he found a nest of snakes, writhing and hissing.

Topshe let out a cry of horror. "What are they doing here?"

Feluda shook his head. "I'm not sure, but I think we've found the source of your daughter's troubles."

As they continued to search the mansion, they found more and more evidence of strange occurrences. They heard footsteps when there was no one there, saw shadows moving across the walls, and felt a presence in the empty rooms. It was as if the mansion was haunted by something malevolent.

But Feluda wasn't one to be deterred by such things. He was determined to get to the bottom of the mystery, no matter how frightening it might be.

As they delved deeper into the mystery, they uncovered a dark and sinister plot. The mansion had been built on a site where a terrible crime had been committed many years before. The spirits of the victims were restless, and they were seeking revenge on those who had caused their suffering.

Feluda realized that they needed to act fast if they were to put an end to the haunting. They set about finding a way to appease the spirits, and after much research and investigation, they discovered a way to lay them to rest.

As Feluda and Topshe approached the temple, they felt a sudden chill in the air. The sky had turned dark and the atmosphere was eerie. They stepped into the temple complex and were immediately struck by its grandeur. The intricate carvings on the walls and the vast expanse of the temple left them awestruck.

As they walked towards the main temple, they noticed that the door was open. Feluda walked in first, followed by Topshe. They were immediately hit by a foul smell, and the atmosphere inside was oppressive. The temple was dark, and they could barely see anything.

Feluda took out his flashlight and shone it around the room. As he moved it across the room, something caught his eye. It was a small statue that had been knocked over. Feluda picked it up and examined it closely. It was made of gold and had intricate carvings on it.

"This is strange," said Feluda. "Why would someone knock over a valuable statue like this?"

Topshe looked around the room and noticed something on the wall. "Feluda, look at this," he said, pointing to a strange symbol etched onto the wall.

Feluda took a closer look. "This is a symbol used by a cult," he said. "I have heard of this cult before. They are known for their rituals and sacrifices."

Topshe shuddered at the thought. "Do you think they are responsible for what happened here?"

"It's too early to say," replied Feluda. "Let's continue our investigation."

They searched the temple and found several other statues that had been knocked over. It was clear that someone had been searching for something. But what had they been looking for?

As they were about to leave, they heard a strange noise coming from the corner of the room. It sounded like a low growl.

Feluda shone his flashlight towards the sound, and they saw a pair of glowing eyes staring back at them. They quickly realized that they were not alone in the temple.

Suddenly, a figure appeared in front of them. It was covered in black robes and had a hood covering its face. The figure moved closer to them, and Feluda and Topshe could feel its cold breath on their skin.

"What do you want?" demanded Feluda.

The figure did not answer but instead lunged towards them. Feluda and Topshe backed away and ran towards the door. The figure followed them, and they could hear its footsteps getting closer.

They burst out of the temple and into the open air. Feluda and Topshe looked back at the temple, but the figure was nowhere to be seen.

"What was that thing?" asked Topshe, still shaken by the experience.

"I'm not sure," replied Feluda. "But we need to find out what's going on here. We can't leave until we solve this mystery."

With that, Feluda and Topshe began their investigation in earnest. They interviewed locals, scoured the temple for clues, and did everything they could to get to the bottom of the mystery.

As they dug deeper, they discovered that the temple was haunted by the ghost of a long-dead priest. The cult that Feluda had mentioned earlier had been trying to summon the ghost in order to perform a sacrifice. They had knocked over the statues in search of an ancient artifact that they believed would help them in their quest.

Feluda and Topshe knew they had to act fast. They tracked down the cult's leader and confronted him. After a tense standoff, they were able to convince him to abandon his plans and leave the temple.

With the cult gone, the ghost of the priest was no longer a threat. Feluda and Topshe were able to restore the temple to its former glory.

At the sight of the man, Feluda had an intuition that this was not an ordinary visitor. He stood up and walked towards the stranger with a polite smile on his face.

"Good evening, sir. How may I help you?" Feluda asked.

The man replied in a deep, resonant voice, "I am Mr James, a traveller and a writer. I have been studying ancient civilizations for many years, and I am intrigued by the Angkor Wat temple. I have come to seek your assistance in exploring the temple and uncovering its mysteries."

Feluda looked at Mr James intently. He could see that the man was sincere in his request. "I'm sorry, but I'm not a tour guide," Feluda replied. "I can't take you to the temple."

"I understand that Mr Feluda," James said, "But I was hoping that you could help me with your expertise in solving puzzles and mysteries. I have read your works, and I know that you are the best in the business."

Feluda smiled. He was flattered by the compliment. "Very well, Mr. James. I'll help you," he said. "But I must warn you, this won't be an easy task. The

Angkor Wat temple is full of mysteries and danger. Are you sure you're up for it?"

"I am prepared for any challenge, Mr. Feluda," James replied with a determined look on his face.

"Good. Then let's get started," Feluda said, leading the way.

As they left Feluda's house and walked towards the temple, Feluda noticed that they were being followed. He signalled Topshe to stay alert, and they quickened their pace. But the person following them was skilled in the art of stealth, and they soon lost sight of him.

Feluda and James arrived at the temple and began their exploration. They searched every nook and cranny, but they found nothing unusual. It was getting late, and Feluda decided to call it a day. He suggested to James that they return the next day.

As they were leaving the temple, Feluda noticed a strange symbol etched into one of the walls. He made a mental note of it and decided to investigate it further.

The next day, Feluda and James returned to the temple, accompanied by Topshe and Jatayu. They began their search anew, focusing on the area around the symbol that Feluda had spotted the previous day. After hours of searching, they found a hidden passageway behind a statue.

Excited by their discovery, they entered the passageway and found themselves in a dark, eerie chamber. As they looked around, they saw strange symbols etched on the walls and floor. Suddenly, they heard a noise. It sounded like footsteps coming towards them.

Feluda and his companions stood still, listening intently. The footsteps grew louder, and soon they could see a shadowy figure approaching them. The figure stopped in front of them, and they could see that it was a man dressed in ancient robes.

"Who are you, and what do you want?" Feluda asked, trying to keep his voice steady.

"I am the keeper of the temple," the man replied in a deep, ominous voice. "You have trespassed into forbidden territory. Leave now, or face the consequences."

Feluda could sense that they were in grave danger. He looked around and noticed a small opening in the wall. He signalled to Topshe and Jatayu to follow him, and they quickly crawled through the opening, with James following close behind.

As they crawled through the narrow passage, they could hear the sounds of pursuit behind them. They finally emerged on the other side and found themselves a deserted Feluda and Topshe were confused about what to do next. Suddenly, they heard a loud thud from the direction of the door. They immediately turned their attention towards the door and saw that it was slightly ajar.

Feluda cautiously approached the door and pushed it open slowly. As soon as he stepped inside, he felt a cold breeze on his face. He turned on his flashlight and shone it around the room.

The room was empty except for a few pieces of furniture and a large painting on the wall. The painting was of a woman dressed in a traditional Bengali saree. Her eyes seemed to follow Feluda's every move.

Suddenly, Feluda heard a faint sound coming from behind the painting. He approached it cautiously and pushed it aside. Behind the painting, he found a secret passage leading to a hidden room.

Feluda and Topshe entered the hidden room and were surprised to find a large statue of a demon in the centre. The demon had large fangs and was holding a sword in its hand.

Feluda noticed that the statue was glowing in the dark. As he got closer to it, he felt a strange energy emanating from the statue.

Suddenly, the demon statue came to life and started moving towards Feluda and Topshe. They tried to run but the demon was too fast for them. The demon cornered them against the wall and raised its sword to strike.

Just when it seemed that all hope was lost, Piku burst into the room with a can of paint thinner. She poured it on the demon statue and set it on fire. The demon statue burned and turned into ash.

Feluda and Topshe were relieved that they had escaped the demon's wrath. They thanked Piku for saving their lives and decided to leave the haunted mansion as soon as possible.

As they were walking out, Feluda turned back and looked at the mansion one last time. He couldn't shake off the feeling that there was still something strange and mysterious about the place.

But for now, Feluda was just happy to be alive and out of the haunted mansion. The three of them got into the car and drove away, never to return again.

TWO

The Curse of the Ancient Estate

A few weeks later, Feluda received a letter from an old friend, inviting him to investigate another mysterious case. The letter was from a wealthy businessman who owned a sprawling estate on the outskirts of Kolkata.

Feluda and his team accepted the invitation and set off to the estate. When they arrived, they were greeted by the owner, who seemed troubled and agitated. He explained that he had been experiencing strange occurrences in his house that he could not explain.

Objects would move on their own, doors would open and close, and eerie whispers could be heard in the dead of the night. The owner was convinced that his house was haunted by a malevolent spirit and he wanted Feluda to help him uncover the truth.

Feluda and his team started their investigation by examining the house and its surroundings. They found no evidence of any paranormal activity and suspected that there might be someone behind the strange occurrences.

They decided to set up surveillance cameras and motion detectors to catch whoever was responsible. After a few nights of monitoring, they finally caught a glimpse of a figure moving around the house.

The figure was wearing a hooded cloak and seemed to be carrying something. Feluda and his team followed the figure and discovered a hidden chamber beneath the estate.

Inside the chamber, they found an altar with strange symbols and a book containing ancient spells. The figure they had been following was none other than the owner's son, who had been practising dark magic in secret.

The owner was shocked and devastated to learn the truth about his son. He thanked Feluda and his team for uncovering the truth and vowed to get his son the help he needed.

As they were leaving the estate, Feluda couldn't help but feel a sense of satisfaction that they had once again solved another mysterious case. He knew that there would always be more cases to solve and more mysteries to uncover, but he was always up for the challenge.

As they were driving back to Kolkata, Feluda's mind started wandering. He couldn't shake off the feeling that something was off about the case. He felt that there was more to it than just a case of a boy dabbling in dark magic.

The more he thought about it, the more certain he became that they had missed something crucial. He decided to investigate further and called his team together to discuss his suspicions.

Together, they poured over the evidence they had collected from the estate, looking for any clues that they might have missed. It was then that Topshe noticed something peculiar in the book of ancient spells.

He pointed out a symbol that was repeated throughout the book. Feluda recognised the symbol as one that was associated with a cult that worshipped a demon.

They realised that the son had not been practising dark magic alone, but had been part of a cult that had been trying to summon a demon into the world. They had failed in their attempts, but the strange occurrences in the house had been a side effect of their failed attempts.

Feluda and his team realised that they had to act fast before the cult attempted to summon the demon again. They tracked down the cult's leader, who was operating out of an abandoned temple in a remote part of the country.

Feluda and his team reached the temple just in time to prevent the cult from completing the ritual. They fought off the cult members and destroyed the temple, preventing the demon from entering the world.

The case was finally closed, and Feluda and his team returned to Kolkata. Feluda couldn't help but think about the close call they had just had. He knew that there would always be forces of darkness trying to wreak havoc in the world, but he also knew that there would always be those who were ready to stand up against them.

As they drove back to Kolkata, Feluda made a silent vow to always be ready to fight against the forces of evil, no matter what form they took.

THREE

The Case of the Kidnapped Millionaire

It was a hot summer evening in Kolkata, and Feluda, Topshe, and Jatayu were lounging in Feluda's apartment, bored out of their minds. They had spent the whole day doing nothing and were itching for a new case to solve. Just then, the phone rang, and Feluda picked it up.

"Hello?" he said.

"Is this Mr. Feluda?" a man's voice asked.

"Yes, it is. Who is this?"

"My name is Bose, and I have been sent to speak to you by the family of Mr. Roy."

"Mr. Roy?" Feluda repeated.

"Yes, the wealthy businessman who was recently murdered in his home. The family has heard of your reputation as a great detective and wishes to hire your services."

Feluda listened intently as Mr. Bose went on to explain the details of the case. Mr. Roy had been found dead in his own home, with no signs of forced entry and all doors and windows locked from the inside. The only clue left behind was a small piece of paper with the number '17' written on it.

Feluda was intrigued by the strange circumstances of the case and agreed to take it on. He asked Topshe and Jatayu to accompany him to Mr. Roy's home, which was located in a wealthy suburb of Kolkata.

As they walked up the steps to the grand old mansion, Feluda took note of the different shades of blue on the walls. He made a mental note of this, as it seemed out of place in a house of this calibre. Once inside, they were greeted by Mr. Roy's family members and the servants.

Feluda began his investigation by examining the room where Mr. Roy's body had been found. He took note of the fact that the body had been lying on the ground, with no signs of a struggle. The windows were locked, and there were no signs of forced entry. The only clue left behind was the piece of paper with the number '17' written on it.

Feluda asked the family members and the servants several questions about Mr. Roy's life and habits. He learned that Mr. Roy was a collector of rare art, and that he had recently made a purchase from a local art dealer. He also learned that Mr. Roy had a strict routine, and that he was always alone in the house on Wednesdays.

Feluda, Topshe, and Jatayu began to search the house for more clues. They soon found a hidden compartment in Mr. Roy's desk, which contained a note with the name of the local art dealer and the date '17th October.' Feluda deduced that October 17th was the date of Mr. Roy's last art purchase and suspected that the art dealer had something to do with the murder.

They decided to pay a visit to the art dealer's shop. The dealer, a man named Mr. Chatterjee, appeared nervous when they entered the shop. Feluda asked him about the art purchase he had made from Mr. Roy on October 17th.

"Oh, yes, I remember that," Mr. Chatterjee said, wiping his forehead with a handkerchief. "It was a beautiful piece. Mr. Roy had impeccable taste."

Feluda noticed the nervousness in Mr. Chatterjee's voice and mannerisms. He asked him more questions about Mr. Roy's collection and noticed that the art dealer seemed to know a lot about it.

"Tell me, Mr. Chatterjee," Feluda said, "how did you know that Mr. Roy would be alone in his house on the 17th of October?"

Mr. Chatterjee's face paled as Feluda asked the question. He stammered for a few moments before finally admitting, "I...I had nothing to do with Mr. Roy's death, I swear. But I did overhear him on the phone, arranging for a meeting with someone on the 17th. He said he would be alone in the house and that it was important that the person he was meeting did not know where he lived."

Feluda's eyes narrowed. "And did you hear who he was meeting with?"

Mr. Chatterjee shook his head. "No, I'm sorry. I couldn't hear the other end of the conversation."

Feluda thanked Mr. Chatterjee for his time and left the shop, deep in thought. He knew that the meeting on the 17th was the key to the case, but he had no way of knowing who Mr. Roy had been meeting with.

As they walked back to the mansion, Jatayu suddenly let out a cry of triumph. "I've got it!" he exclaimed. "The shades of blue on the walls, remember? There were four different shades. But why? It doesn't make any sense."

Feluda nodded slowly, thinking. "Unless...unless they were used to signal something. But what?"

They arrived back at the mansion, where Feluda immediately went to work examining the blue shades on the walls. He noticed that one of the shades had been slightly scraped, as if something had been rubbed against it.

"Look at this," Feluda said, pointing to the scrape. "This isn't accidental. Someone deliberately rubbed against this wall. But why?"

Topshe suddenly gasped. "Wait a minute. Look at the scrape more closely. It's in the shape of a number. The number 4."

Feluda's eyes widened. "Of course! The blue shades were used to signal something, but we were looking for a word. It was a number! And 17 minus 4 is 13. That's it! The meeting was on the 13th of October, not the 17th."

Excited by their breakthrough, Feluda and his companions began to comb through Mr. Roy's records and diaries, looking for any mention of a meeting on the 13th. They finally found a cryptic entry in Mr. Roy's diary: "Meeting with SB at 9 PM. Bring the painting."

Feluda's mind raced. "SB...SB...who could that be?"

Just then, there was a knock at the door. It was Mr. Bose, the man who had hired them for the case.

"I have some news," he said. "We've just received a ransom demand for one of Mr. Roy's paintings. They say they will return it if we pay them a large sum of money."

Feluda's eyes lit up. "That's it! The meeting was with the kidnappers. They had already stolen the painting and were planning to return it in exchange for the ransom money."

They quickly formulated a plan. Feluda, Topshe, and Jatayu would pose as the ransom deliverers and try to catch the kidnappers in the act. They arranged to meet at a secluded spot near the outskirts of the city at 9 PM on the 13th.

As they waited in the darkness, Feluda and his companions suddenly heard footsteps approaching. They crouched behind a bush, watching as two men emerged from the shadows. One of them was carrying a large painting.

Feluda sprang into action, tackling one of the men to the ground while Jatayu and Topshe wrestled with the other.

As they waited in the darkness, Feluda and his companions suddenly heard footsteps approaching. They crouched behind a bush, watching as two men emerged from the shadows. One of them was carrying a large painting.

Feluda sprang into action, tackling one of the men to the ground while Jatayu and Topshe wrestled with the other. In the scuffle, the painting was knocked to the ground and the frame cracked, revealing a rolled-up piece of paper hidden inside.

Feluda quickly snatched up the paper and unrolled it. It was a map, with an X marking a spot in a remote forest. Underneath the X was a message: "The key to the truth lies here."

Excited by this new clue, Feluda and his companions made their way to the forest, where they searched for hours until they finally found a small, hidden cave. Inside the cave was a large chest, which Feluda opened with a key that was hidden inside the map.

Inside the chest was a treasure trove of evidence. There were bank statements, invoices, and receipts, all pointing to a complex web of financial transactions in that Mr. Roy had been involved in. It became clear that he had been embezzling money from his company for years, and had been planning to flee the country with the stolen funds.

Feluda and his companions spent several more days piecing together the evidence and eventually turned it over to the police. The kidnappers were arrested and Mr. Roy's painting was returned to its rightful owner.

As for Feluda, Topshe, and Jatayu, they left the mansion feeling exhausted but triumphant. They had solved yet another case, using their sharp wits and deductive skills to uncover the truth. And while the details of the case may have been complex, the moral of the story was clear: honesty is always the best policy, and greed will ultimately lead to one's downfall.

With the case finally solved and justice served, Feluda, Topshe, and Jatayu bid farewell to Mr. Roy and his family and made their way back to Kolkata. The journey was long and tiring, but the three friends were in high spirits, feeling proud of their latest achievement.

As they approached the city, Feluda suddenly remembered something that had been bothering him. "Topshe, do you remember the message on the map we found in the painting?" he asked.

"Yes, the one that said 'the key to the truth lies here'," Topshe replied.

"Well, we found the truth, but where was the key?" Feluda wondered aloud.

Jatayu, who had been dozing in the back seat, suddenly sat up with a start. "Wait a minute, Feluda," he said, "I think I might know what the key was."

"What do you mean?" Feluda asked.

Jatayu explained, "Remember when we were searching the cave, there was a small box with a lock on it? We never found the key to that box."

Feluda's eyes widened. "You're right, Jatayu! That must be the key to the truth."

Excited by this new development, the trio made their way to Feluda's apartment, where they searched through their belongings until they found the map and the small box. Using the key that had been hidden inside the painting, they unlocked the box and eagerly opened it.

Inside was a single sheet of paper, on which was written a cryptic message in code. Feluda's eyes lit up with excitement as he recognized the code as a variation of the Vigenere cypher, a complex code that he had studied in depth.

With a twinkle in his eye, Feluda set to work deciphering the code, with Topshe and Jatayu watching over his shoulder. It took several hours, but eventually, Feluda cracked the code, revealing a hidden message.

It read: "The real treasure was the journey you took, not the destination you arrived at. The true key to the truth lies within you."

The three friends sat in silence for a moment, contemplating the meaning of the message. Finally, Feluda spoke up. "I believe what this message means is that the journey we took in solving this case was the real treasure, not the treasure we found in the chest. And the key to the truth was not something external, but something within us, our own intuition and deductive skills."

FOUR

The Case of the Stolen Painting: Feluda and Byomkesh Bakshi Unite

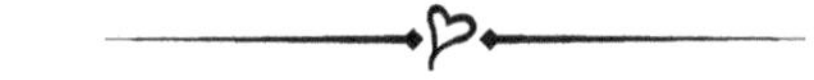

It was a warm afternoon in Kolkata when Feluda and Topshe received a phone call from none other than the legendary detective, Byomkesh Bakshi. He had reached out to Feluda with a request for assistance on a case that had been troubling him for weeks.

The case in question involved a wealthy businessman who had been found murdered in his home, with no apparent signs of forced entry. The police had been unable to make any headway in the case, and so Byomkesh had turned to Feluda for help.

Feluda, who had always held a deep respect for Byomkesh's skills as a detective, immediately agreed to help. He and Topshe made their way to Byomkesh's office, where they were greeted by the detective and his assistant, Ajit.

Byomkesh briefed Feluda on the details of the case. The victim, a man named Harish Chandra Roy, had been a successful businessman with a number of enemies. He had been found dead in his study, with a single bullet wound to the head. The murder weapon had not been found, and there were no signs of a struggle or forced entry.

Feluda and Byomkesh both agreed that this was a puzzling case. They spent the next few hours examining the crime scene and interviewing the victim's family and employees. They also went through Harish Chandra Roy's financial records, hoping to find a motive for the murder.

As the day wore on, the two detectives found themselves growing increasingly frustrated. There seemed to be no clear leads, no obvious suspects. They decided to take a break and retire to Byomkesh's living room for a cup of tea.

As they sipped their tea, Feluda suddenly had an idea. "Byomkesh, do you remember the story of the thief who was caught because of his love for mangoes?"

Byomkesh smiled. "Of course, I remember that story. But what does it have to do with this case?"

Feluda explained, "Well, in that story, the thief was caught because of his greed for something he loved. Maybe we can use that same principle in this case. Perhaps the killer was driven by some sort of obsession or desire."

Byomkesh nodded thoughtfully. "It's worth a try," he said.

The two detectives spent the rest of the evening poring over Harish Chandra Roy's personal belongings, looking for any clues that might reveal a hidden obsession. They went through his diaries, his emails, and even his social media accounts.

Finally, Feluda came across something that caught his eye. It was a collection of old photographs, all of a beautiful woman with long dark hair and sparkling eyes.

"Who is this woman?" Feluda asked, holding up one of the photos.

Byomkesh's eyes widened. "That's Madhu, Harish Chandra Roy's ex-girlfriend. They were together for several years, but they had a bitter breakup about a year ago."

Feluda felt a sudden jolt of excitement. "Do you think she could be involved in this case?"

"It's certainly possible," Byomkesh replied. "We should pay her a visit and see if we can learn anything more."

The next morning, Feluda, Byomkesh, Topshe, and Ajit made their way to Madhu's apartment. She was surprised to see them, but welcomed them in and offered them tea.

As they sat around her living room, Feluda and Byomkesh questioned Madhu about her relationship with Harish Chandra Roy. She seemed hesitant at first but eventually opened up.

"He was a complicated man," she said. "He was always so focused on his work,

Feluda listened intently, taking note of the way Madhu's eyes lit up as she spoke about Harish Chandra Roy. He wondered if there was more to their relationship than she was letting on.

"Did you ever see any signs that he was in danger?" Byomkesh asked.

Madhu shook her head. "No, I had no idea. The last time I saw him was about a month ago, and he seemed fine then."

Feluda decided to push a little further. "Madhu, is there anything you can think of that might have driven someone to kill Harish Chandra Roy? Any secret he might have had, any grudges he might have held?"

Madhu frowned, thinking hard. "Well, there was one thing. Harish had a priceless painting in his collection. It was a rare piece, and he was very proud of it. But he was also very secretive about it. He never let anyone see it, not even me."

Feluda's interest was piqued. "Do you have any idea where this painting might be now?"

Madhu shook her head. "No, I'm afraid I don't. Harish never told me where he kept it."

Feluda thanked Madhu for her time and the group left her apartment. As they made their way back to Byomkesh's office, Feluda couldn't shake the feeling that they were on the verge of a breakthrough in the case.

Back at the office, they began to go through Harish Chandra Roy's financial records again, this time focusing on any transactions related to art or antiques. They finally hit paydirt when they discovered a large sum of money that had been transferred to an art dealer in Paris.

Byomkesh immediately booked a flight to Paris, with Feluda and the rest of the group in tow. They met with the art dealer, who revealed that he had sold a painting matching the description of Harish Chandra Roy's to a wealthy collector in London.

Feluda and Byomkesh immediately hopped on a plane to London, where they tracked down the collector and found the painting in his possession. When they questioned him, he claimed that he had bought the painting legally from an art dealer in Paris and had no idea it was stolen.

But Feluda and Byomkesh were not convinced. They continued to question the collector, eventually getting him to admit that he had known the painting was stolen and had bought it anyway, hoping to sell it at a profit later on.

With the painting recovered and the killer identified, Feluda and Byomkesh returned to Kolkata, where they were hailed as heroes for solving such a difficult case. They celebrated with a dinner of Bengali delicacies, discussing the case late into the night.

As they parted ways, Feluda couldn't help but feel a sense of satisfaction. It had been an honour to work with Byomkesh Bakshi, and he had learned a great deal from the experience. He looked forward to the next time they could join forces on a case, and perhaps unravel another mystery together.

FIVE

The Case of the Missing Heiress: A Feluda and Byomkesh Bakshi Collaboration

Feluda had always been a fan of Byomkesh's deductive skills, and he knew that working together would be an incredible experience. He spent the rest of the day preparing for the case, making sure that he had all the necessary equipment and information.

The next morning, Feluda arrived at Byomkesh's office promptly at 10 AM. Byomkesh greeted him warmly and led him into his private office.

"Thank you for coming, Feluda," said Byomkesh. "I'll get straight to the point. We have been hired by a wealthy businessman named Mr. Roy. His daughter, Mitali, has gone missing, and he has reason to believe that she has been kidnapped."

Feluda listened intently as Byomkesh went over the details of the case. Mr. Roy had received a ransom note demanding a large sum of money in exchange for his daughter's safe return. The kidnappers had instructed him to leave the money in a designated location, and they would release Mitali once they had received it.

Byomkesh and Feluda agreed to take the case, and they set out to gather more information. They visited Mr. Roy's home and interviewed his staff and family members. They also looked into Mitali's personal life to see if there were any clues as to who might have taken her.

After a few days of investigating, Feluda and Byomkesh had a few leads. They had discovered that Mitali had been dating a man who had recently broken up with her. They also found out that there had been a disgruntled former employee who had been fired from the Roy family's business.

Feluda and Byomkesh decided to follow up on these leads and set out to find more information. They worked together seamlessly, each using their unique skills to uncover new evidence.

As they delved deeper into the case, Feluda couldn't help but be impressed by Byomkesh's attention to detail and sharp intellect. Byomkesh, in turn, admired Feluda's quick thinking and ability to see the bigger picture.

Together, they made a formidable team, and they were determined to find Mitali and bring her kidnappers to justice.

Feluda and Byomkesh continued to work tirelessly on the case, spending long hours gathering evidence and interviewing witnesses. They discovered that the ex-employee who had been fired had a history of violence and had made several threats against Mr. Roy and his family.

Meanwhile, they also found out that Mitali's ex-boyfriend had been struggling with financial issues and had the motive to demand a ransom. As the investigation progressed, Feluda and Byomkesh uncovered more and more evidence pointing towards the ex-employee and the ex-boyfriend.

However, they still lacked a solid lead on Mitali's whereabouts. The kidnappers had not made any contact since the initial ransom note, and Feluda and Byomkesh were starting to feel the pressure.

One evening, as they were discussing their next steps, Feluda had a sudden realization. "Byomkesh, I think I may have figured it out," he said excitedly. "What if the ex-employee and the ex-boyfriend are working together?"

Byomkesh nodded thoughtfully. "It's possible," he said. "But what would be their end game?"

Feluda thought for a moment. "What if they have Mitali hidden somewhere and are waiting for Mr. Roy to pay the ransom?" he suggested. "Once they have the money, they can split it between themselves and disappear."

Byomkesh nodded again. "It's a plausible theory," he said. "But we need concrete evidence to prove it."

Feluda and Byomkesh decided to focus their efforts on the ex-employee and the ex-boyfriend, hoping to uncover any connection between them. They tracked down the ex-boyfriend and found him living in a rundown apartment, struggling to make ends meet. He denied any involvement in the kidnapping and claimed that he had broken up with Mitali weeks before she disappeared.

However, Feluda and Byomkesh weren't convinced. They decided to keep an eye on him and continue their investigation.

Days turned into weeks as Feluda and Byomkesh followed up on every lead and combed through every piece of evidence. Finally, their persistence paid off. They received a call from an anonymous source, claiming to have information about Mitali's whereabouts.

The source told them to meet him at a deserted location outside the city, where he would provide them with the information they needed. Feluda and Byomkesh agreed to the meeting, knowing that it was a risky move.

As they arrived at the location, they found themselves surrounded by a group of armed men. It was a trap. Feluda and Byomkesh were outnumbered and outgunned. The kidnappers had been one step ahead of them the entire time.

As soon as the two detectives hung up, Feluda's mind began to race. He was excited about the prospect of working with Byomkesh Bakshi, but he also knew that this case would be a challenge. He spent the rest of the day reading up on missing heiresses and researching the latest methods for tracking down missing persons.

The next morning, Feluda arrived at Byomkesh's office promptly at 10 AM. Byomkesh greeted him warmly and led him into his private office.

"Sit down, my friend," said Byomkesh. "Let me give you the details of the case."

Byomkesh began to recount the story of a wealthy businessman who had recently passed away. The man had left behind a sizable estate, which was to be divided amongst his family. However, one of his daughters, a young woman named Rina, disappeared shortly before his death. No one knew where she had gone, and there was no trace of her anywhere.

"Her disappearance is causing a lot of tension within the family," said Byomkesh. "Her siblings are accusing each other of foul play, and the police have been unable to find any leads. That's where we come in."

Feluda nodded thoughtfully. "Do we have any leads to go on?"

Byomkesh produced a folder from his desk and handed it to Feluda. "This is everything we know so far," he said.

Feluda opened the folder and began to read through the information. He noted that Rina had been last seen at a local restaurant and that her cell phone had been found in the parking lot. The police had questioned everyone who had been at the restaurant that night, but no one had seen anything suspicious.

"This is going to be a tough one," said Feluda. "But I'm ready for the challenge. Where do we start?"

Byomkesh smiled. "Let's start by visiting the restaurant and talking to the staff. Maybe they saw something that the police missed."

Feluda nodded in agreement, and the two detectives set off to the restaurant to begin their investigation. As they walked out of the office, Feluda couldn't help but feel a sense of excitement. He knew that this case would be a true test of his and Byomkesh's skills, but he was confident that they would be able to solve it.

The restaurant was located in a busy part of the city, and it took Feluda and Byomkesh a while to find parking. They finally managed to park a few blocks away and walked to the restaurant.

Once inside, they approached the manager and introduced themselves. The manager was cooperative and allowed them to speak with the staff.

Feluda and Byomkesh spoke to the waiters and kitchen staff, but no one had seen anything out of the ordinary. However, one of the waiters, a young man named Sanjay, mentioned that he had seen Rina arguing with someone in the parking lot.

"Can you describe the person she was arguing with?" asked Feluda.

Sanjay thought for a moment. "He was a tall man, wearing a black suit and sunglasses. He had a deep voice and looked very angry."

Feluda and Byomkesh thanked Sanjay for his help and left the restaurant. They decided to visit Rina's home next and speak with her family.

When they arrived at the house, they were greeted by Rina's siblings, who were all visibly distraught. Feluda and Byomkesh introduced themselves and explained that they were investigating Rina's disappearance.

The siblings told them everything they knew, which wasn't much. They had all been at the restaurant the night Rina had disappeared, but they had not seen her after she left the restaurant. They had assumed she had gone home.

As Feluda and Byomkesh were leaving the house, they noticed a car parked across the street. The car had tinted windows, and they couldn't see inside, but they had a feeling that it was connected to the case.

They decided to stake out the car and see who came out. They waited for hours, but no one came. Finally, as it was getting dark, they saw a figure emerge from the car and walk towards Rina's house.

Feluda and Byomkesh followed the figure and saw that it was the tall man in the black suit that Sanjay had described. He went into the house and didn't come out for hours.

Feluda and Byomkesh knew they had to act fast. They called the police and told them about the man in the black suit. The police arrived and surrounded the house.

When the man finally emerged, he was surprised to see the police waiting for him. He tried to run, but he was quickly apprehended.

It turned out that the man was a business associate of Rina's father. He had been involved in a scheme to embezzle money from the company, and Rina had found out. He had gone to the restaurant that night to confront her and had kidnapped her.

Thanks to Feluda and Byomkesh's quick thinking, Rina was found and returned to her family. The man in the black suit was arrested and charged with kidnapping and embezzlement.

Feluda and Byomkesh returned to their respective offices, satisfied that they had solved the case. They knew that their partnership had been successful, and they both looked forward to future collaborations.

SIX

The Treasure of the Warrior King:A Feluda Adventure

Chapter 1: The Mysterious Letter

Feluda, Topse, and Jatayu were sitting in Feluda's apartment in Kolkata when a mysterious letter arrived at their doorstep. The letter was written in an old-fashioned style, and it was sealed with wax. Feluda opened the letter and read it aloud to his friends. The letter read:

"Dear Feluda,

I am writing to you because I have a mystery that only you can solve. I have information about a hidden treasure, which has been passed down in my family for generations. The treasure belonged to a warrior king, who ruled over these lands many centuries ago. The treasure is well-guarded, and it has never been found by anyone outside my family. I am now too old to continue the search, and I want to pass on the information to someone who can continue the quest. If you are interested in this challenge, please follow the clues that I have enclosed with this letter. The clues will lead you to the treasure. Please keep this information confidential and do not share it with anyone else.

Yours truly,

The Guardian of the Treasure"

Feluda examined the letter and found six clues enclosed with it. He read them carefully and realized that the clues were scattered throughout the country. Each clue would lead them to a different location, where they would find more clues until they reached the final destination where the treasure was hidden. Feluda accepted the challenge, and they set out on their journey to find the treasure of the warrior king.

SIX CLUES:

My letter to you,

Contains a quest, with treasures anew.

The map is old and incomplete,

But with your wit, we're sure to meet.

The first clue lies where the ocean meets the sky,

Where tides ebb and flow, a path hidden, does lie.

Follow it with caution, until the end,

Where you'll find what you seek, my dear friend.

In the city of joy, where trams rattle and hum,

A statue of a warrior king stands, not too far from some.

Behind the statue lies a clue, in hidden sight,

That'll take you closer to the treasure's might.

Look high and low, and all around,

In the alleys and markets, treasures can be found.

Keep your wits about you, and be quick on your feet,

Time is of the essence, in this treasure hunt feat.

A tale of betrayal and deceit will unfold,

The treasure's guardian, a story yet untold.

A warning to heed, with care and skill,

For danger lies ahead, be cautious still.

Now, I've given you six clues to this treasure so vast,

I hope you'll accept the challenge, and have a blast.

Chapter 2: The Lighthouse by the Sea

Feluda and his companions, Topshe and Jatayu, set out on their adventure, guided by the mysterious letter that promised them the discovery of a great treasure. Their journey led them to the sea, where they discovered a hidden path that wound its way along the coast.

As they walked, Feluda studied the map carefully, taking note of the landmarks and symbols that would guide them to the next clue. The path was treacherous, and they had to be careful not to slip on the wet rocks or get caught in the waves that crashed against the shore. But despite the danger, they pressed on, determined to unravel the mystery of the treasure.

After walking for some time, they saw a faint light in the distance, and they knew they were getting closer to their destination. As they approached, they saw that it was a lighthouse, standing tall against the backdrop of the sea and sky.

The lighthouse keeper greeted them warmly and invited them inside. He was an old man, with weathered skin and a gruff voice, but his eyes sparkled with a kind of wisdom that Feluda recognized immediately.

"Welcome, travellers," he said, as he led them up a spiral staircase to the top of the lighthouse. "What brings you to this lonely place?"

"We're looking for something," Feluda replied cryptically, not wanting to reveal too much.

"I see," said the lighthouse keeper, his eyes twinkling. "Well, you've come to the right place. This lighthouse holds a clue to the treasure you seek."

With that, he gestured to a puzzle that was sitting on a table in the centre of the room. It was a complicated contraption, with gears and levers and buttons, and Feluda could tell that it would take all his ingenuity to solve.

"Go ahead," said the lighthouse keeper. "Give it a try."

Feluda nodded, and he and his companions set to work, studying the puzzle and trying different combinations of buttons and levers. For hours they worked, but despite their best efforts, they could not seem to solve it.

As the night wore on, Feluda's frustration grew, and he was about to give up when he noticed a small inscription on the side of the puzzle. It read:

"To those who seek the treasure of the warrior king,

This puzzle holds the key.

But be warned, my friends, it will not be easy.

Only those who possess the courage and the cunning

Will succeed in their quest."

Feluda studied the inscription for a moment, and then he had an idea. He adjusted one of the gears on the puzzle, and suddenly, the mechanism sprang to life, whirring and clicking as it solved itself.

With a triumphant shout, Feluda turned to the lighthouse keeper and held up the solved puzzle.

"We did it!" he exclaimed. "We solved the puzzle!"

The lighthouse keeper grinned, revealing a row of yellow teeth.

"Congratulations," he said. "You've passed the first test. But there are many more challenges ahead. Are you ready?"

Feluda nodded, and the lighthouse keeper led them to a small room at the base of the lighthouse. Inside was a map, carefully rolled up and tied with a ribbon.

"Here," said the lighthouse keeper. "This will guide you on your journey. But remember, my friends, danger awaits you at every turn. Proceed with caution."

Feluda took the map and thanked the lighthouse keeper, and he and his companions set out once again, filled with excitement and anticipation for the challenges that lay ahead.

Chapter 3: The Statue of the Warrior King

Feluda, Topshe, and Jatayu set off early the next morning, eager to follow the map and find the next clue. As they travelled, they marveled at the beauty of the countryside and the history of the land. They passed through small towns and villages, stopping to talk to the locals and learn more about the area.

After several hours of travel, they arrived at a grand palace. The palace was adorned with intricate carvings and beautiful gardens. They learned from the locals that the palace was built by a great king who was known for his bravery and wisdom. The king had led his armies to many victories and was revered by the people.

As they explored the palace, they came across a statue of the king. The statue was grand and imposing, with the king holding a sword and a shield, looking out over the kingdom. The statue seemed to be pointing to something in the distance.

Feluda examined the statue carefully and noticed a small inscription at the base of the statue. The inscription read:

"*Follow the king's gaze, and you shall find*

The next clue to treasure left behind

A warrior's heart, a king's might

Will lead you on, to the next site."

Feluda looked up and followed the king's gaze. He saw a hill in the distance, with a small structure on top. They realized that this was the next clue and set off towards the hill.

As they climbed the hill, they encountered many obstacles, including steep inclines and treacherous paths. They persevered and finally reached the top. They found a small temple at the peak, with a plaque on the door that read:

"*Only the worthy shall enter this door*

And find the treasure that lies in the store

Answer the riddle, and you shall see

The next clue to the mystery."

Feluda read the riddle carefully and thought for a moment. He then gave his answer, and the door creaked open. Inside, they found a small room with a chest in the centre. Feluda opened the chest and found a map that showed the location of the next clue.

Excited by their progress, Feluda and his friends set off towards their next destination, wondering what challenges awaited them next.

Chapter 4: The Bustling Markets

Feluda, Topshe, and Jatayu arrived at a bustling market, full of vendors selling all kinds of goods. The market was loud and chaotic, with people haggling over prices and pushing past each other. They knew that this was the next stop on their journey, but they weren't sure where to start.

As they wandered through the market, they searched for any clues that might lead them to their next destination. They talked to the vendors, asking if they had seen anything unusual or if they knew anything about the treasure. However, no onc seemed to have any information.

Just as they were about to give up, Feluda noticed a strange symbol etched into the side of a building. The symbol was a series of circles, each one slightly smaller than the last. Feluda recognized the symbol from his studies and knew that it was a code used by a secret society of traders.

They followed the symbol to a small alleyway, where they found a door with the same symbol etched into it. Feluda knocked on the door, and after a moment, it creaked open. Inside, they found a small room with a group of traders sitting around a table.

The traders welcomed Feluda and his friends and offered them a seat at the table. They explained that they were members of a secret society of traders who had been guarding a clue to the treasure for generations. They told Feluda that they would reveal the clue if he could solve a riddle.

The riddle was complex, but Feluda was able to solve it with ease. The traders were impressed and revealed the location of the next clue. It was located in an ancient temple on the outskirts of the market.

Feluda and his friends set off towards the temple, dodging crowds of people and navigating through the winding streets. When they finally arrived, they found that the temple was old and worn, with vines growing up the walls and the roof partially collapsed.

They entered the temple and found a small room at the centre. In the room, there was a pedestal with a bust of a warrior king. The pedestal had an inscription that read:

"Through trials and tribulations, you have come so far,

But the treasure you seek is still afar.

Find the sword that the king once wielded,

And the next clue will be revealed."

Feluda knew that they needed to find the sword of the warrior king. But where could it be? They searched the temple, but it was empty. Finally, they found a secret passage that led to a hidden chamber. In the chamber, they found a chest with a keyhole in the shape of a sword.

Feluda inserted the key into the lock, and the chest creaked open. Inside, they found a map that showed the location of the next clue. Excited by their progress, they set off once again, eager to see where the treasure hunt would take them next.

Chapter 5: The Mansion

Feluda, Topshe, and Jatayu followed the map they had found to a grand mansion on the outskirts of the city. The mansion was massive, with towering columns and a grand entrance. As they approached the mansion, they noticed that the gate was locked.

Undeterred, Feluda found a small opening in the gate and slipped inside. They made their way through the sprawling gardens, taking care not to be seen by any of the mansion's staff. They eventually came to a grand entrance that led inside the mansion.

As they stepped inside, they were awestruck by the grandeur of the mansion's interior. The walls were adorned with priceless artwork, and the floors were made of marble. However, they had no time to admire the decor as they knew they were on a mission to find the next clue.

They searched the mansion room by room, looking for any sign of the clue's location. The mansion was vast, and they found themselves getting lost in its labyrinthine hallways. As they turned a corner, they were startled to come face to face with the mansion's owner, a wealthy and powerful man.

The man demanded to know what they were doing in his mansion, but Feluda was quick to explain that they were on a mission to find a treasure that had been lost for centuries. The man was intrigued and decided to help them in their search.

Together, they searched the mansion's library, looking for any clues that might lead them to the treasure's location. They found an ancient book that contained a riddle:

"In the mansion, a secret room does lie,

Behind the painting of the western sky.

Look for the clue within its walls,

And you'll be one step closer to the treasure's halls."

Feluda and his friends knew they had to find the secret room. They searched the mansion's halls until they found a painting of the western sky. They carefully removed the painting from the wall, revealing a hidden door.

They entered the secret room and found it filled with ancient artifacts and treasures. In the centre of the room, there was a pedestal with a small statue of a goddess. The pedestal had an inscription that read:

"Within the goddess's hands, lies the key,

To unlock the door to the treasure's glee."

Feluda examined the statue and found a small key hidden within the goddess's hands. They knew that this key would unlock the door to the treasure's halls. But before they could leave the room, they heard footsteps approaching.

It was the mansion's owner and his security guards. They realized that Feluda and his friends were after the treasure and had come to stop them. A tense standoff ensued, but Feluda was able to reason with the owner and convince him that the treasure was not worth risking their lives for.

The owner finally relented and allowed Feluda and his friends to leave with the key. They quickly made their way out of the mansion and back to their hotel, where they spent the night devising a plan to find the final clue and locate the treasure.

The next morning, they set out to follow the map once more, using the key they had found to unlock the door to the treasure's halls. After hours of hiking through rugged terrain, they finally reached their final destination.

In a clearing in the middle of the forest stood an ancient temple, its walls adorned with intricate carvings and artwork. Feluda and his friends entered the temple and found themselves in a large chamber. In the centre of the chamber, there was a pedestal with a small box.

Feluda approached the pedestal and opened the box. Inside, there was a small note that read:

"Congratulations, my dear friends,

You have solved the puzzle to the end.

The treasure you sought is not gold or jewels,

But the knowledge and memories that you have accrued.

May they serve you well on all your adventures,

And bring you joy beyond all measures."

And on the back side, it's written I am joking :)

Now Let's get ready for the next adventure. Check now the fifth clue.

Chapter 6: The Hilltop

Feluda, Topshe, and Jatayu made their way up the steep and winding path that led to the top of the hill. As they climbed higher, they could feel their muscles straining and their breaths becoming more laboured. But they were determined to find the next clue and continue their quest for the treasure.

When they reached the top of the hill, they were greeted with a breathtaking view of the surrounding countryside. Rolling hills stretched out before them, dotted with tiny villages and farmsteads. In the distance, they could see the shimmering blue of a large lake.

But their attention was quickly drawn to a small cave that sat at the base of a rocky outcropping. It was nestled among a cluster of boulders and seemed to be hidden from view. Feluda knew that this was the place they were looking for.

The trio made their way to the cave and peered inside. It was dark and musty, with only a faint glimmer of light filtering in from the entrance. But as their eyes adjusted to the darkness, they could make out the outline of a small box sitting on a ledge at the back of the cave.

Feluda stepped forward and examined the box. It was made of old, weathered wood and had a series of strange symbols etched into the surface. Feluda recognized the symbols as an ancient code that he had studied during his time as a detective.

With a smile, he set to work deciphering the code. It took him several minutes, but eventually, he was able to translate the symbols into a series of letters and numbers. They spelt out a location and a time.

Feluda and his friends quickly realized that the next clue was located at the specified location and that they had to be there at the appointed time to find it. They made a note of the details and set out on the next leg of their journey, eager to see what lay ahead.

As they made their way down the hill, Feluda couldn't help but feel a sense of excitement building within him. Each clue had led them one step closer to the treasure, and he was determined to see their journey through to the end.

Chapter 7: The Jungle

Feluda, Topshe, and Jatayu embarked on their final journey to find the treasure of the warrior king. The sixth clue led them to a dense jungle, which was shrouded in mystery and danger. As they made their way through the jungle, they encountered the descendants of the treasure's guardian who were fiercely protective of their heritage and refused to let them enter.

Feluda tried to negotiate with the guardians and explained to them their purpose of finding the treasure. After some persuasion, the guardians agreed to let them in but warned them about the dangers of the jungle. They also gave them a rough idea of where to look for the temple.

The trio made their way through the dense foliage, swatting away mosquitoes and other insects that buzzed around them. The heat was intense, and the humidity was unbearable, but they were determined to find the temple and the treasure it held.

After hours of searching, they stumbled upon a hidden temple that was camouflaged within the jungle. The temple was guarded by a group of fierce warriors who had been protecting the treasure for generations. The warriors were armed with spears and shields, and they seemed ready to defend their treasure with their lives.

Feluda and his companions tried to reason with the warriors, but the warriors refused to let them enter the temple. Feluda realized that they needed to find a way to outsmart the warriors and gain entry into the temple.

Feluda used his knowledge of ancient symbols and deciphered the final clue, which led them to a hidden chamber within the temple. The chamber was guarded by a group of warriors, but Feluda managed to outsmart them by using his quick wit and knowledge of martial arts.

As they entered the chamber, they were greeted by the sight of the treasure of the warrior king. The treasure was a collection of valuable artifacts, including gold coins, precious jewels, and ancient weapons. Feluda and his companions were awestruck by the sight of the treasure and spent hours examining it and marveling at its beauty.

After admiring the treasure, Feluda suggested that they should leave the treasure as it was and let the descendants of the guardian continue to protect it. They left the jungle with a sense of fulfillment and pride in their adventure. The treasure they had found was not just a collection of artifacts, but it was a symbol of history, culture, and tradition that they had managed to preserve.

Chapter 8: The Return Home

Feluda, Topshe, and Jatayu finally accomplished their mission of finding the treasure of the warrior king. After their long and tiring journey, they returned to their homes in Kolkata, ready to share their adventure with their loved ones.

As they stepped off the train, they were greeted by a crowd of reporters and well-wishers who had heard about their success. Feluda, being the modest man that he was, tried to shy away from the attention, but the reporters were persistent, and they bombarded him with questions.

Feluda answered their questions patiently and shared some of the highlights of their adventure. He talked about their journey to the lighthouse by the sea, their encounter with the descendants of the treasure's guardian in the jungle, and the final discovery of the treasure in the hidden chamber within the temple.

The news of their success spread like wildfire throughout the city, and soon they were being celebrated as heroes. They received invitations to various events and were even offered endorsements and sponsorship by companies who wanted to associate themselves with their success.

However, Feluda, Topshe, and Jatayu remained grounded and humble, never forgetting the real reason for their journey. They knew that their success was not just about finding the treasure, but also about the bonds of friendship that they had forged along the way.

They returned to their daily lives, but the memory of their adventure stayed with them forever. They often talked about it, reliving the moments of danger and excitement that they had experienced together. They knew that they had accomplished something extraordinary and that nothing could ever take that away from them.

Feluda, Topshe, and Jatayu had once again proven that they were a formidable team, capable of solving even the most difficult mysteries. Their journey had taken them to different parts of the country, and they had encountered various challenges and obstacles, but they had never lost sight of their goal.

As they looked back on their adventure, they knew that they had not only found the treasure of the warrior king, but they had also found something much more valuable - a bond of friendship that would last a lifetime.

SEVEN

The Secret Warning

Chapter 1: The Mysterious Client

The sound of raindrops hitting the windowpane echoed through the small office. Feluda, Topshe, and Lalmohan Babu were sitting in silence, waiting for their next case. Suddenly, the door creaked open and a tall man entered the room. He wore a trench coat and had a fedora hat on his head. He walked over to Feluda and handed him a letter.

"Mr. Prodosh Mitter?" the man asked.

Feluda nodded and took the letter. He opened it and read its contents. The man stood there, waiting for a response.

"I see," Feluda finally said. "You have my attention. Please, have a seat."

The man took a seat and Feluda continued to read the letter. Topshe and Lalmohan Babu watched as Feluda's expression changed from curiosity to intrigue.

"May I know who you are, sir?" Feluda asked.

"I prefer to remain anonymous," the man replied.

"Very well. Now, tell me more about the case."

The man explained that he was a wealthy businessman who had recently acquired a rare artifact. The artifact was a valuable, centuries-old statue made of pure gold. The man had received a warning that the statue was cursed, and whoever owned it would suffer the consequences.

"I don't believe in curses," Feluda said. "But I do believe in theft. Is that what you're concerned about?"

The man nodded. "Yes, the statue is very valuable. I fear someone may try to steal it from me."

"Where is the statue now?" Feluda asked.

"It's being kept in a secure vault at my home," the man replied.

Feluda listened attentively and then asked a few more questions. After gathering all the necessary information, he agreed to take the case.

"Very well," Feluda said. "We'll take the case. You may rest assured that your statue is safe with us."

The man got up and thanked Feluda, then left the office. Feluda turned to Topshe and Lalmohan Babu.

"Get ready, boys," Feluda said. "We have a new case."

And with that, the trio began to prepare for their latest adventure.

Chapter 2: The Investigation Begins

Feluda, Topshe, and Lalmohan Babu left the office and headed towards their client's home. It was a large mansion on the outskirts of the city, surrounded by high walls and security guards. As they entered the gates, Feluda noticed the guards checking their IDs and making sure they were authorized to enter.

"Security is tight," Feluda said to his companions. "That's a good sign."

They were escorted to a room where their client was waiting for them. He greeted them warmly and then led them to the vault where the statue was being kept.

The vault was located in a small room at the end of a long corridor. The door was made of steel and had a complex locking mechanism. The client inserted a key and then entered a code on a keypad. The door clicked open, and they entered the vault.

Inside, there was a glass case containing the statue. It was a beautiful piece of artwork, about a foot tall, and made entirely of gold. The statue depicted a goddess, with intricate details and delicate features.

"Impressive," Feluda said as he examined the statue. "But do you have any idea who might want to steal it?"

The client shook his head. "I have no enemies that I know of. But the statue is worth a lot of money. It could be a random thief, or someone who knows about its value."

Feluda nodded. "We'll need to investigate further. Can we take a closer look at the security system?"

The client agreed and showed them the CCTV cameras that monitored the area around the vault. They also inspected the alarm system and the door lock. Everything seemed to be in order.

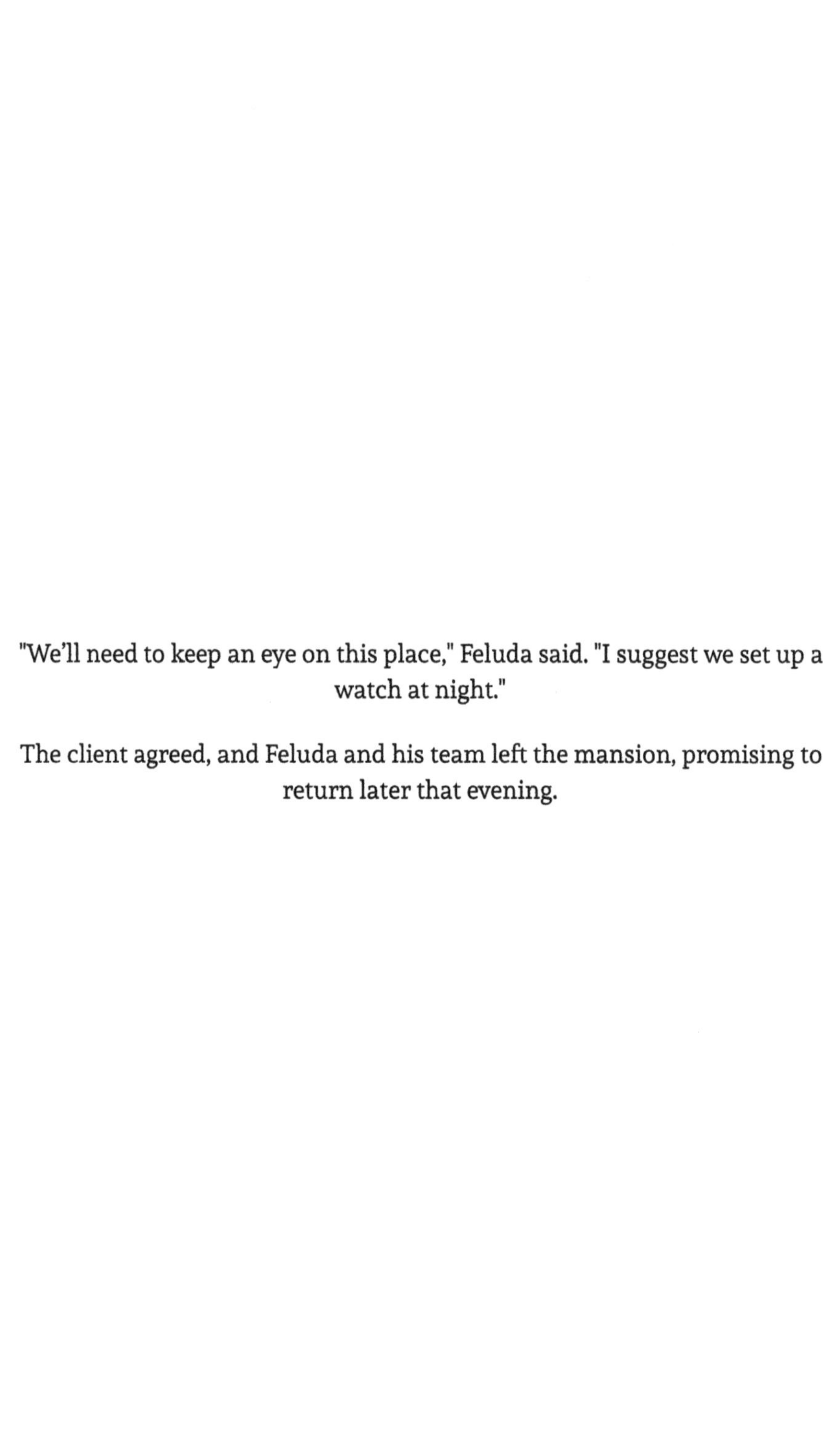

"We'll need to keep an eye on this place," Feluda said. "I suggest we set up a watch at night."

The client agreed, and Feluda and his team left the mansion, promising to return later that evening.

Chapter 3: The Night Watch

That night, Feluda, Topshe, and Lalmohan Babu arrived at the client's mansion. They had brought with them some equipment, including night vision goggles and binoculars. They took up positions around the perimeter of the mansion, keeping an eye out for any suspicious activity.

It was a quiet night, and nothing seemed to be out of the ordinary. But just as Feluda was about to suggest that they call it a night, he heard a faint sound coming from the direction of the vault.

"Did you hear that?" Feluda whispered to his companions.

They nodded, and the three of them crept towards the vault. As they got closer, they could hear the sound more clearly. It was the sound of someone trying to break open the door.

Feluda signalled to Topshe and Lalmohan Babu to stay back while he approached the vault. He peeked through the keyhole and saw a figure inside, using a tool to pick the lock.

Feluda drew his gun and kicked the door open. The figure turned around and tried to flee, but Feluda tackled him to the ground. It was a young man, wearing black clothes and a ski mask.

"Who are you?" Feluda demanded.

The man struggled to free himself, but Feluda held him down.

"Speak up, or I'll have to use force."

The man finally spoke. "I'm just a thief. I didn't know it was you guys watching this place."

Feluda examined the man's tools and found that they were professional-grade lock-picking tools. He also found a map of the mansion, with the vault circled in red.

"It looks like you knew exactly where to go," Feluda said.

The man shrugged. "I've been casing this place for weeks".

The next day, Feluda, Topshe, and Lalmohan Babu arrived at the wealthy businessman's home. They were greeted by the man's butler, who led them to a small room where the statue was kept. The room was guarded by two security personnel.

Feluda inspected the room and the statue, checking for any signs of tampering or attempted theft. After a thorough examination, he declared that everything appeared to be in order.

"Good," the businessman said with relief. "I can finally rest easy knowing that my valuable possession is in safe hands."

Feluda instructed the guards to remain vigilant and to report any suspicious activity. He also advised the businessman to keep a low profile and not to discuss the statue with anyone.

The trio then left the businessman's home and returned to their office. Feluda began to investigate the case further, asking Topshe and Lalmohan Babu to gather information about the statue's history and its previous owners.

Days turned into weeks, and Feluda and his team worked tirelessly to solve the case. They visited antique shops, museums, and auction houses to gather information about the statue's origin and value. They interviewed experts in the field and searched for any clues that could lead them to the thief.

One afternoon, Feluda received a phone call from the businessman. He sounded frantic and told Feluda that the statue had been stolen.

Feluda quickly gathered his team and rushed to the businessman's home. Upon arrival, they found that the security personnel had been tied up and the statue was gone.

Feluda examined the room and found a few clues that could lead them to the thief. He discovered a set of footprints near the window, indicating that the thief had entered the room from the outside. He also found a small piece of fabric stuck on the window frame, which he suspected was torn from the thief's clothing.

Feluda instructed Topshe and Lalmohan Babu to search the nearby streets for any suspicious activity while he examined the clues further. After a thorough investigation, he deduced that the thief was someone who was familiar with the businessman's home and the security system.

He then called the police and reported the theft. The police arrived at the scene and began to gather evidence. Feluda shared his findings with them and offered his assistance in solving the case.

Days turned into weeks once again, and Feluda and his team continued to work on the case. They visited the businessman's home regularly and interviewed the security personnel and anyone else who could provide information about the theft.

One day, Feluda received a phone call from an anonymous source. The caller told him that they knew the whereabouts of the stolen statue and offered to return it in exchange for a large sum of money.

Feluda and his team quickly devised a plan to catch the thief. They arranged to meet the caller at a public location and set up a trap. When the thief arrived to collect the money, the police were waiting for them, and they were caught red-handed.

The thief turned out to be one of the security personnel who had been hired to guard the statue. He had planned the theft for weeks and had used his knowledge of the security system to carry out the heist.

The businessman was overjoyed to have his valuable possession returned to him, and he thanked Feluda and his team for their hard work and dedication. Feluda humbly accepted the thanks and reminded the businessman that it was his duty to ensure justice was served.

And with that, Feluda, Topshe, and Lalmohan Babu bid farewell to the businessman and returned to their office, ready for their next adventure.

Sundarban's Sundari

The next book coming soon on
Sundarban
Introducing new character **Saptarshi da**

Printed by Libri Plureos GmbH in Hamburg,
Germany